Earth's Shipping Yard

TODD RYKACZEWSKI

WORD REVOLT, LLC. ATLANTIC BEACH, FL

Earth's Shipping Yard
Chapter One. Part I

Upon arrival there were a few moments that held as a sense of incarceration. First being the lack of temperature in the room. Even though it was light blue there was no feeling of atmosphere. It was as if I was standing in a sealed plastic lunch bag or small Tupperware container made especially for vegetables. Not so much for carrots but for weaker stock like tomatoes or sliced cucumbers.

The area was not very large but there was also no intellect of a boundary. A person standing here could feel like they might walk on forever but had knowledge that distance was irrelevant. The second moment was the lack of white noise. Not a moment's rest from the hum of one's own analytical mind could be conjured. If there were units of electricity those units had been well insulated or killed. Bringing to question the source of the light. All light bulbs gave off white noise at some hearing ability. Maybe, I had gone deaf, immune or ambivalent.

Then there was the loss of time. How long had I been standing here thinking about the moments that have distracted me from the only important question, where am I? "Ah yes," said a voice from all directions. "Where are you indeed!?" Continued the endogenous voice. You might be over there or here or maybe under a rock but definitely not anywhere near the moon. It might be a possibility that you are in one place and your mind another. Let's both think about the latter question and all the possibilities in depth and get back to each other someday."

With a long chasing silence the voice was absent. The nothingness was once more a resident chamber for one. An unavailable location that didn't feel like a prison but had the same opportunity for overthinking. With nothing to be had there were only past experiences and The Voice, to inhale, exhale then choke over due to the lack of oxygen and content. The only joy came from the generous light that stagnantly hung as atmosphere rather than beams of color or lack thereof. Shades had conquered sight without eyewear and conjured like a mob of protesters in front of a kneeling recruit. Thick and airy more than mud there came a feeling of standing in the middle of a smoke stack rather then stuck in bed. Although, this was not the solitude of a dream mixed with lucid cravings for sleep. This moment had energy, poison rushing the body to move on a mental stage that existed in ransom moments that were forced to pay remembrance to life. A past life but a life none the same or similar.

Left wondering the question about how this candle lit body flamed and flickered as transient, right past an average long life? Why were the quiet times so forgettable while the loudness blind?

Is it so unearthed to think that we have special moments? Those chips of time genetically linked to family and those who are fleshly marked in friendship. Capable of forging together just out of being sticky situations? For how short the season of growth grows do we hesitate in any transition towards the love we have felt for those travelers rangled in a similar path as our own? Is there room for hesitation or pause to calculate the hours we have lived as a branch on a stick that started to grow before we were even an idea?

Before the mind could formulate a shadow that would be left to reason out the past, The Voice returned to remark, "Mothballs! All of you might be here but the majority of Them are luminaries. If it helps, plant any sorrows you're the only one of Them who is physically here, that's why the room is yours without trespassers. Consider yourself on layaway, not quite ready to be purchased but if everything goes well outside of this room, you might be picked up."

Tired of games that rang neutral without being monotone, discomfort tossed like an itch on the neck when the nerves misdiagnose the irritant as a spider instead of the wind. There could no longer be this peace that hung like unimaginative clouds representing nothingness, not even a turtle or ship. It's rigorous to contemplate alone but to have an invasive voice that interrupts only to add chaos rather than a cup of tea was maddening not to mention the daring monologue about those that I loved. How could a simple tone know the location of those that had been common and myself that had not been forgiven?

"Whatever might be this space, a cloud or dream and maybe a stroke, tell me one answer! Relative to elevation where is it that we stand? How high or low are the conversations of this dialogue? Am I being robbed or guiled into rage through guilty trial?! Do we or you great Voice have any conclusion to the condition of this one way relationship that might be preceded as cruel guidance? You, if you are a You, sound as a noise of reason but even the kind fall harem to such mistrust.

Tell me great icebreaker of the cloudy environment and tell me fast with little pride or hidden rhyme. Why do you appear and then die out coldly just as the seasons or a deranged life not certain of Their warrant from authority. Is there a reason to hide under perfect conditions or might there be laziness that wins in a prison that lacks air and wind? Are you too an inmate? Incarcerated in a zip lock bag that has no movement but only time to push fluttering souls? Capsulated without gravity in a moment that loves nothing but floating the issue. Where weightlessness comes to terms with waiting only to describe time spent harboring power that is represented without knocking on a door.

So I stand, you great Voice of the stainless that lingers on while the intrusion of the yesteryears wane in as little bits of unanswered heartbreaks. Where are They, where is my wife!? What happened to my dog Fox? Are my parents okay? Finally, the last lingering question oh great Voice, are my friends doing fine? Who is looking after Them all while I stand in this room arguing with myself and you! A Voice that is most likely fictional. Where did They go? Where did Them go? Those, Theirs, Ours, Yours? How is it that I'm alone in a plastic box without any recollection about the arrival?"

Perplexed, there never came a quick response. Stranded in stance the time we are familiar with moved on. People were born, died, did great accomplishments and ultimately left them behind. In truth, the standing alone was not the worst part but feeling alone was. The conscious knew there was more going on in life than what had appeared to be. Unengaged, forgotten, the years of an average life went by. Fifty years to be exact. If there was dust to be collected there would have been a fine layer in complex forms around what stood in waiting that might as well be an antique in Earthly years but remained young here. On hold never looked so good on the charts of a loving spouse.

Frozen in thought. My wife had to have gone through elder times by herself. It's not like time existed in this void or even hair growth to point out the passing of flesh. Purpose paused to protest any imagery that resembled progression of those stuck in a particular age category. Exactness of nothing made each wondering question land and dissipate on the time that came before.

In many ways this all could have just been one order of coffee and I soon would emerge to the task of clearing out the gunk from my eyes followed by a brisk brushing of the teeth. The only difference is in my bedroom there would be my wife and a few of my teeth in the back are chipped. Running a quick tongue check my teeth, they felt perfect. Ah, so this is not reality, a simple dream to confuse the night and play tricks on a brain robbed of its sight. With the matter of where and why settled all there was to do was to find a spot to sit and wait out the vertical rest. Sitting down with no stress from argumentative bone warmers the decent was enjoyable for someone my age. Planted on nothing but lower than previous and still with the same forever view I started to think about breakfast. Bacon, toast with jam, mushrooms baked with cream cheese in the middle! Yes, I'll have the mushrooms and…. Slicing that warm thought in half The Voice that was trying too hard to sound serious came back.

You will not have the mushrooms with cream cheese in the middle

You will not have bacon

You will not have toast with jam

You will stand up and forget about breakfast!

A little confused but then the idea that it might be Sunday and in which case I normally sleep through breakfast and start with lunch.

"Stand now," said The Voice. Sitting comfortably I figured that there really wasn't anything a Voice could do to me but be annoying. Sorry loudspeaker but your demands are mute to my pleasurable state.

A little louder and with more testosterone The Voice regurgitated the previous two words. Stand Now. As I seemed to have time, our dialogue continued with no wins or repercussions on either side. Towards the end we were in a great ballet of two stubborn dancers standing or sitting in a compromising way by our present faults. The Voice didn't have a body and I was confused in contempt. Just as water evaporates into the clouds only to fall back down the two of us were powerless over the other described best by a guitar and strings.

If I stood The Voice would only stop until I sat back down. Both secretly unwilling to compromise we played on. At first this was amusing, comforting and useful. Every time The Voice said to stand up I would count the time in between. Thirty one seconds, The Voice made a demand every thirty one seconds. Now, I could keep track of time in effort to figure out the conclusion to this entrapment. Helping greatly to block out the tyranny of mortal questions that held my peace hostage. The Stand Up clock gave structure to an unmallaeble world that held no edges but spanned only the distance of my arms reaching out. At five foot eleven that was not very far.

The clock now rang to announce the fifth hour of my protest. Never thought I would hold a sit-in during a dream but here I was trying to stick it to the ultimate voice pushing an unwanted, possibly deserving demand. The pleasure had now removed itself from the drama while hostility took quarter in its place. The Tupperware container felt cooler with a darker shade forming just beyond the nothingness. Stand Up, grew lower with an obvious increase in vibrancy. The Voice had gone far enough as well and the moment our dual would end with a loser pushing to the point we had turned into bullies. This banter of back and forth was not playful in recollection as it was a way to cage awareness of existence. We both were simply fighting each other through ourselves.

"Stand up," chimed the faceless monster living with me in the endless now. It had been fourteen hours plus the time that went uncounted. Fourteen hours and then some, I have had no control over my body, not kissed my wife or knew what it felt like to be on Earth experiencing cool winter wind just before Thanksgiving while our dog Fox hopped through the woods acquiring ticks that he would later give to us in bed that night watching a movie. All gone. The only sense left was sight and sound. Outside of that my memories were given the task to refresh my mind about the human touch, smell then pain. There I stood as a toy doll in a well lit box with no price on my packaging. "Stand up" marked the twentieth hour of sitting. Quickly in this experiment being asleep had been ruled out. Coma, maybe but why The Voice? Why the nothingness? With an underlying condition of being mad at the healthcare system in America the idea that all of this was brought upon through generic drugs being pumped into my system while being charged for name brand. Still, until there is a doctor prescribing wine I'll always boast a complaint.

The Voice and I went on for seven more years. At some distant point we both calmed down and we just went through the motions. The pitch of the now gregarious request chimed on with a mocking sensation of air hitting a window pane in another room. Our contempt dried out to an almost pure white. Memories faded the taste of my wife's lips after eating an orange popsicle. Now, we hung low in a sober celebration of both sides being the victor. What we had won and the cost didn't stand trial to how we felt. The voice and I were inevitably the same. Both stuck without a body that would evoke change. Yes, I could sit or stand and move through a continuum, but to what point? So The Voice could ring as a child or thunder like a hug but again to what point? All this time we spent fighting had come to the conclusion that we were merely distracting each other from what was really going on. Why was I a human stuck in a box with a voice? With a deep breath that wasn't associated to stiffness considering I'd been sitting for nine years, I stood up.

The voice rang "Stand Up!"

I had already been standing at this point. Replying, "Look again my well calculated friend, it's over, you won. I'm now vertical. A great pause that lasted much longer then 31 seconds rained some denial over my choice to give in and exist the way The Voice wanted. Now there returned the oblivious notion of not knowing how much time was going by but what it felt like was certain. Years and in a lot of ways the majority of another lifetime. Then another lifetime and another. Still standing but with time without interaction from The Voice to break up the loneliness. I would spend eighty years standing and the next sitting. Without the feeling of hunger my only worries came in as forgetfulness.

Each life time I would forget time spans that were drenched with those that offered family. The love grew smaller with each decade. Days became a cleansing ceremony for the precious recollection that made a person smile to themselves in the grocery store as They rediscovered a particular food. The demolition of my past was set. The only thing I could do now was stand in representation of an old mall losing one store at a time. Soon my mind would be vacant besides a few older people using the indoor air conditioners to get a power walk in before, after and during a rainstorm. Less popular stores went first, like Chinese apparel, kids jewelry, a teenage tattoo shop that used to be a vitamin store, prom dresses, 80s pleather furniture and finally hot pretzels. Leaving only a few coin rides and abandoned vending machines. Even the store where my wife found her wedding ring that didn't need sized because we had been destined to be together from day one. Soul mates, or travelers through time that had always no matter what found the other in any period of history.

Oh, the nights we would talk about who we were in other lives. Pirates that sailed a green ship called Fern after the island we commandeered the boat from that was home to fern farmers. Long nights playing a Victrola while drinking illegal whiskey in a speakeasy we built under our home just for the two of us, with the exception of a wondering soul or two.

Even the times we were poor, lost kids to a plague and even died chasing some youthful dream. Her and I did it all and that all had kept me going through this moment. Now, there was no holding on to any of that. A few more generations stuck in this box and I will have lost her memory all together. Yes, our kids mattered but they will never be their mother on a pirate ship in the open seas.

The last store in the mall just locked their door for the final time. It has now been another estimated 300 years. When I think of somebody I can only think of me and The Voice. I know They might have existed at some point but who cares? It's only me and the bossy clock that matters. "Stand Up," chimes the keeper.

"You stand up!" I yell. Sitting back down from excitement as the count begins again. One, two, thirty one and we both yell at the same time Stand Up we have now organized a pattern. With nothing left on my end and nothing to begin with on the voices end we have decided to merge the madness. I stand, then sit and wait for the jack in the box to arouse movement. I was nothing and I was everything to that Voice in need of me to direct. Friends, partners in the nothing that was this never molding moment. After all of this we were not fighting but learning each other's language.

The Voice didn't want to control but to orchestrate our every move together as one unit. A family of give and receive and, "stand up." Yes, I now completely understand who I am in a plastic box wrapped in blue cloth. I'm dead, tucked away under my wife's bed. The voice steadily replied, "Stand up."

I couldn't do much. The psychotic wave of energy had passed with a short feeling of shimmer. Sunshine and orange peels burnt then landed forgotten in compost that failed to yield in the winter. Most of life failed to go the way of the harvest in the colder months. Some grasses would grow all the way to the point the Earth froze but that might not even be true. Hopefulness flossed the blank slate that now grabbed at the abstract. Nothingness, a mind will build in effort to keep the other bodily functions working.

After all, if I'm sane there's room to eat and feel motivated to chase the happy feelings. Only Issue is there are no longer the recollections hanging in the drying barn. That barn had fallen down years ago and the wood mulched for playgrounds. The only part remaining is the piece of timber that lays twenty feet below the cement slab that holds Walmart in place. Sitting back down while trying to clear the rant that ruled my arms on their mission of flopping around while twitching.

One idea had to be cleared. Why was I once again remembering my wife and what makes me think I'm dead? After all, anyone would forget everything at this length of only having themselves and a repetitive voice to communicate with. Some would say that there are stages of emotions when the morgue rotates through the mind as a realistic outcome along side going to the grocery store or digging a hole in a garden.

At this point the depression had faded and acceptance in the form of defeat came rolling in with a seize. Who I had been or would have been now was little more than a few stories wrongfully told by new generations trying to piece together their ancestry. Stuck in the waiting room of life while being truly forgotten and wondering why anything happened or would happen from here on out.

Breathing even slower at this point the signs of a waning body became clear. From here there was nothing to look at but vast nothingness. Nothing to hear but the sound of crisp cotton clothing folding from rare movement. Taste had hitch hiked a ride with smell on the back of the fact that there was no air. Stagnant stature stole hollowed care that sang a lullaby to a carcass too willing to die. A few blinks of the eye passed in an hour only to turn into hours with a few blinks of an eye. After that, time had consented with its victory. With no sense to distinguish my individuality, I went blind. The mind was the last to cease function but went the quietest. A speck of white paint on a giant wall now represented the passing of this continuum.

Dialogue that ran flickered in effort to persuade the fire to embrace the future ash it would become. It being the soul or possible last connection to humanity. For when there would only be a body sitting unresponsive to any chemical reactions there would be a hollowed stump left in ultimate space to dry out through eternity. In many ways, explaining how lonely a life some will be dealt is too much to withstand. With that noted there were three more times I would breathe. The first inhale was to say goodbye to all of those who I loved on Earth. The second intake made clear that my intentions were always to love my wife. Last lung expansion went past in pilgrimage to what might be considered religion.

Chapter One. Part II

In most scenarios there are conclusions to the events that take part on our journey around the sun. A tree grows until it's wood or fertilizer for the greater good. Mountains fall into smaller bits of rock. Glaciers in this time frame melt into the oceans then placed into plastic bottles.

As old as time society has demanded an explanation for when anything ends, especially loved life. The antiquated question, why do we lose our loved to the ground? Future scientists that are left to explain the reasoning behind Earth's destruction will ultimately come up with a few simple reasons or how we trashed our planet. Scientist One: The people have long destroyed the Earth because they had to dispose of their loved ones and grief into six foot holes they called graves. By placing that much sorrow down through the soil they unconsciously grew angry at Earth. Over time there were too many places of grief and not enough understanding of the conclusion of life, they decided to end the ritual of being human and killed the planet.

The Scientist would go on to write this collection of findings and turn their ideas in to the colleges around the world in search for a form of validation. They would title the papers, *The Buried Earth Effect*. The process of killing off the planet so there's no longer a need to bury a loss. This would also happen on other future colonies.

Then again, we do tend to not take care of what we feel like is not ours or what we did not earn. Leaving the room big enough for a second chair for another hypothesis. Scientist Two: Homosapiens of the past killed off Earth due to the easy notion that They no longer owned it. Through taxation, low wages, violence and law They simply felt captive to the work week that slowly expanded into seven days instead of five. Providing just enough fried chicken to get them through until the next shift. They, Them, Those and Us did not possess anything so the collective did not host a green care. In the end the population fantasized about the fall of society while envisioning about the rebirth of nature over infrastructure. Scientist Two would call Their report, *Returning Home.* An exploration of not owning your planet and the effects on the consumer enslaved residents.

Both Scientists would eventually agree on one conclusion and that was the need for a finale. Yes, the requirement of sophistry is a human condition that plagues more than others but lives well when anything attached to life is refreshed. New shoes, a haircut, nail trimming, orgasm, shower or even closing your eyes at night. There is an eternal need for an end. In many cases it's the wrong end but we still cherish the idea that there wouldn't be more until the next time a particular thing or idea was killed.

Unfortunately, there wasn't an end when those three breaths spent their need to express prevalence.

20

Those three human necessities might have changed the story but not the dialogue. For many more centuries I sat as a body in that shipping container just as much of our stuff sits in storage units. The difference here being that this facility was all together abandoned on a road no one had any reason to go down. The land was not valuable or the items worth saving for their intrinsic value.

It would take chance and love at the auction house to free the junk that lined the fleshy chambers waiting to be unlocked. A key had long been a symbol of freedom but in this case was a lost hope. What was needed here would be luck or a crossing of the stars. If only we knew what was needed then there would have been a fast liquidation sale of units but that would be cheating. All of us stacked like Legos had to wait for Them to open the doors.

For thousands of mood swings and millions of rants there was the connotation that I was alone in this great pause. That somehow this never ending condition was special to just me. Like the majority I too even thought death was uniquely my own and that somehow I would go about all of this differently then all the others that traveled a similar timeline. In fact, the container that held what was last seen of me reflected an endless row of similar boxes. In death this place was or would be known as Earth's Shipping Yard. A containment enterprise that was meant to hold all of those who could not move on to another life without their soul mate.

The Shipping Yard
Chapter Two. Part I

This particular extraterrestrial lot was just like
what you might have seen going sixty miles an hour over
a long bridge in a city built by a major ocean. Colorful
containers stacked five to seven feet tall with names from
all over the world printed on the side. Except for being
company names, the painted symbols represented who
was waiting on the inside. Most of the shipping
containers had faded or rusted and a few had fallen in to
disability and decay even for the heavenly. As fast as the
current of time could deliver, vessels were picked up by
the thousands by large autonomous cranes and stacked
on the ground sorted by year. The current year, being
the busiest of the years passed fading in popularity with
the future back in time.

Everything at the yard works without any
employees or staff of human distinction. To describe the
scene would be to tell you to picture a never-ending table
pushed against a forever cliff that faced a perfectly blue
sky. Now, stack a rainbow of boxes on that surface.
There is no distracting sound or winged bird and
definitely not whether to break the process of the efficient
shipping yard. Crates came in processed then set in their
place for what might be an eternity. It was a place to wait
or be forgotten indefinitely, with no help through what
was probably a hard transition. That's how it usually is

though with change, it just happens and you're left to figure out the next moment alone. Even if you're not stranded to a mind's eye you're most always alone in your conscious. In this case thought along with The Voice is all the people trapped in the containers had. Orphans to an unknown debt. Stuck wondering why they had to be and never be while ripening from a human form that had somewhat adjusted into being an undefined idea.

We in the shipping yard could not save ourselves let alone others stored as product and in result reset. Frozen in a place that rarely took orders and out of rule never took customer orders. The original products, the people, had to be the original orders. Otherwise we were sacrificed in the name of our partner's happiness. Collateral damage known as The Unlucky who have to wait to fix their wrong doing but most likely get recycled after the mineral value has decreased enough. Worthless, they're dead, so there is time for that.

At the very end of the shipping yard a timeline came in a dark moment better described as *recycled nobody's*. A place so far down the timeline of humanity that there was no hope for those stuck in this transition. Maybe the world has changed too much or the living one opted to never come back to Earth.

No matter the cause this was that conclusion we talked about earlier. Just in this case their memories would have been so long ago that there wouldn't be much to do but to delete the jail that held someone who was long forgotten.

In short we are all here waiting for the one we love to rescue our shortcomings from our purgatory. I was never a religious person on Earth but in this moment it might have been a good idea to at least be kind. Instead we and everyone else that failed in some way to be a human that cared for others by leaving more than what they had in mind to take.

This shipping yard was not heaven or hell or something twisted in between. We simply did not take care for the attention shown upon us. Like sucking bandits they contained to run like drugstore thieves through an overly harsh place. Our planet was rugged so we gave hard responses back and that is why we in the containers made for material objects facing deletion. We sucked with our soul mates and they moved on because they had choices. Decisions that were only theirs to make without ever taking a second chance on the one that we gave them.

In other words this is why I'm at the shipping yard and my wife, a person in her own right has left me here. You see, when anyone from any religion, from any walk of life meets their soul mate, the universe bonds a contract between them. From there, love for life grows or shrinks. Actions are not recorded but rather intentions. Whoever has lived a fuller life that has benefited the survival of the Earth gets to make the choice. Rescue your soul mate and come back together or try again and come back alone. Alone you'll have free will, if you bring back your soul mate you'll have to change their destructive ways. Obviously the populist chooses to come back stag as they have learned by the time of death that you can't change people, so we are taught through many books that live online as blogs.

There you have it. Stand up had a greater meaning than keeping time. This was not to direct a bodily action but a failure to be kept on the yard any longer. Every time the voice said stand up a person in a designated container was deleted and I was one step, one foot closer to being gone. Stand-up was refreshing to a forgotten individual in that their actions led to the moment they no longer needed to take space in the universe. Every thirty one seconds a mom, dad, brother, husband, wife or teenager was leaving forever and all I could do was think about time.

How much time, seconds, years, generations, I was losing but in reality that voice didn't care. All they cared about was to prepare the end for another one of me. A populator of the common good that raved from tossing coffee cups out along with my gas powered car. Nothing is perfect but idealism can lead to a wrong way of incorrectly preserving motivation.

"Stand up," rang over the nothingness once again. That small fire that had turned into ash found an ember and ignited. We hear the words tossed around the media and assumed they are for ourselves instead of a cry to unite and stop another from going extinct. Stand-up was not an order but a cry from humanity to save the world. If we are not taking action in the form of subtraction then the conclusion should be an end.

Scientists were right that destructive behavior had landed us here but if we are to ever get out of Earth's Shipping Yard there must be a radical way to save those of us who are already here, those who are disappearing because we thought standing up was a way to calculate imprisonment. After all, those of us who are here were the most influencing players in a selected time. Anywhere from the artist using Chinese yellow to the oil drillers and this very typewriter with lead painted gilding.

"Stand up," another four containers shine bright then change from a solid then to nothing that will never be. Another opportunity lost in the space of waiting trillions if not the extent of all-time relating to two-legged creatures continuously tossed overboard in a clarification of the one goal we all hold in common. Surviving the next climate change in effort to rescue the species that will be recorded as the only species that single-handedly destroyed not only their environment but countless others. Still, I would treck to extinction if it were not for one chance encounter that freed me from shipping off the edge.

It was a forgetful time in history where nothing mattered and the media ran politics in the same manner as a child's cartoon. People were all distracted by any means possible rather it be VR, TV or some format having further progressed like internal advertising while we slept. Yes, in 2100 your dreams will run as advertisements. That's if we as a people are here and not fooled to go to Mars while Earth's destruction is completed by the removal of all its resources. There's a hidden reason we are pushed to the stars by those not interested in our hearts but our sense of leaving the mundane. I'll leave that rant for now and return to the first line.

It was a forgetful time in history, when I knew my wife Hayden, where nothing mattered and the media ran politics in the same matter as a child's cartoon. There she stood, my soul mate and future wife reading a book on the possibilities of utopianism while drinking a latte in a foam cup with an asking price of one hour's wages.

This contradiction however was not her doing but out of necessity of caffeine. Being a student, along with shop owner came a high price tag with overwhelming exhaustion that could only be remedied by quick fixes. What she did on her own time took the picker out of the picked.

Her name was Haley but she went by Hayden in favor of the androgynous movement. Sometimes her hair fell short and others reached for knees that resembled the female form in boy jeans. Gender was suggestive at the time and Hayden made it a point to suggest that there should not be a suggestion when it came to that kind of digestion. Sans binary feelings, the idea was exactly what led Hayden from cheerleader to activist. Saving the soldered existence between where popularity ran uncovered and mingled with reality.

Persuasion pronounced refusal in hindsight as a way to commonly reject annunciation as a common practice over irregularity. Who were those that minded the field of the streets and lived in the caves where the ore had resided? Could there ever be cleanliness in a district that lay healthy with a country and state fat from improvisational dialect that warrants no punishment? Would people impeach a leader and worse yet could they muster the matter in the face of eating raw meat?

Hayden lay awake mixing commercial energy drinks with wine that married spirits of fast conclusions. Fierce in a dream the fight never won until the battle came in with leadership only to raise efforts that ran to a bicycle. In Hayden's sleep the regret would yell, stand up! As if her body would be mad at being at rest. At this point we had lost all hope towards emissions. In all honesty, we didn't care. At that time we both did everything, as everyone wanted. Junk tossed its way out of our shop as well as the home at least twice a day.

Who cared? We were rather angered about bearing a dream or that everything we built was rented. Either way there was a clear destiny between the important matters and those that brought up earthy emotions that living made us deal with.

Important matters being rent, food and in there somewhere running our nonprofit. Unimportant causes ranged from pollution or caring for a planet only a few actually had the opportunity to enjoy. In both matters or should I say dealings the outcome would be more or less the same. After all, are we not all headed to Mars?

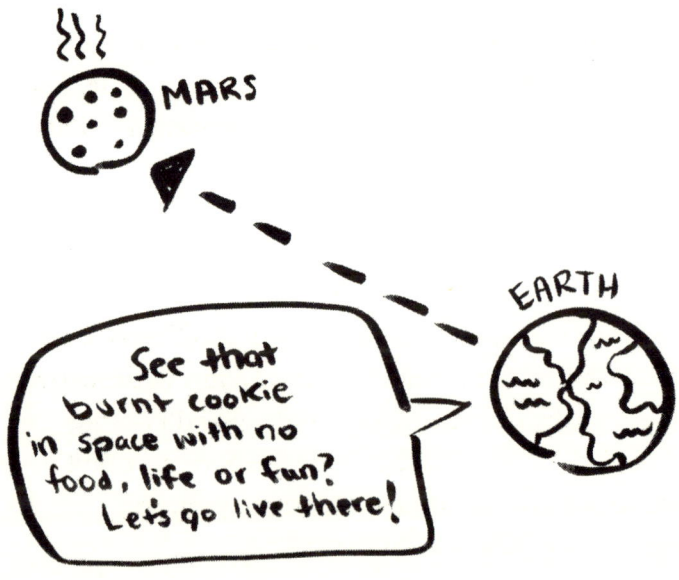

Anyway, in some distant alteration we held a form of coherence that warranted us to start a non-profit. Then, reality split the golden hair. Hayden continued to save the world and I followed a gluttonous path of social media mixed with fame. Sure Hayden was worthy but where was my institution of popularity? Did I not deserve a new phone and all the ringtones promising a form of gratification? Who can afford to be left behind when we've already done our worst!

That's everything I would have said given how this moment makes me look. Truthfully I love Hayden. She loves me. Pushed, I took the job that paid and Hayden saved the world. In reality all I cared about alongside the rest of the world was zombies and the end of times. Hayden on the other hand focused on Utopia. One of us went on to raise free art schools and the other now in a box facing the reason that, "Stand Up," was personal and not global.

The voice now repeats itself every 20 seconds instead of 31. Time is running past reality and sanctuary turns viral in a chronic tragedy. Regret is worn in any weight of a t-shirt but also on the skin. All that is left is inner faith that the wicked will fall in short to the cards handed out by the dealer. Otherwise we will quickly understand the term full hand, as the bodies we laid alongside the works crafted folded to a gun, in representation, fall to a shot again.

A little effort to not run on, this delivery should be clear in exhibiting complaining as a sign of loss of control. In this case where I am compartmentalized there is no control. All of us that have been boxed have no control over anything let alone the workings of Earth. We wait for the voice to judge us when the time comes for our last words. Stand up. Until then we rotate conjectures in the same effort of blinking an eye.

Paralyzed professionals, made in medicine that we write off as medication that is safe only because someone who went to school said it was okay. And so it is. The diagnosis ails our worrisome contributions. Uncertainty abandons our bodies just as it came with no effort. Leaving to question, how do I know about the shipyards? If I was a common prisoner at best, what magnetic relevance is there between two gyros of a humble guard of Earth's malpractice and their keeper? It's like when you buy flowers, do they last the hour or the day? That does not matter. It's who you share hugs with and I hugged Quartz Arkwright just before the arched walkway collapsed between breath number three and Hayden forever.

Quartz Arkwright: Keeper of Containers
Chapter Two. Part II

A corner of the shipping container turned green and a figure emerged in 2D at first then rounded out. There was a short pause to allow for the transition of Their body and my disbelief. Then They spoke, "Let it be known if there is no one that commits me to confront your disabled manner on the forefront of being deleted like your forefathers before you and those mothers before them. We might be in conclusion but the concluded has to stay between our words. You know? Those tiny spaces between wasted ink that some edit while others trash a lifetime producing a format that better suits the aptitude of those mildly wealthy others?

Don't listen but you'll be tried and running dry on inspiration. You would like to know my demeanor, if not own it and yet there is a sacrificial response to the morbid way punctuality gratifies your face. Oh, lost person in a department store box, don't cry. You'll never have to Stand Up as long as you listen. Hear the words you're about to commonly receive."

A slender attribute delivered the latter and in doing so broke my monotony of the voice while saving the third breath from trials of murder. This execution of ideals also empowered mobility that edged on the previous hot ash that might still be enchanted fire. Memories regained ground around what could be resembled as a personality. Quartz being the only visitor in more than enough time, I had to know, why my cubicle? Why my life and in this case why go against the model of standing up?! Their persona existed as a monologue more than a reality. Who cared and in reality why would they bother at all. Quartz was metallic in nature while that nature might be leaden as a lesson. Style on the other hand is left to the upbringing in the natural lands of any civilization that dares to welcome use while willing to reproduce. Quartz started to speak again, "Hey? What is that and what are you fooling around with? Okay, maybe you are silent to a friendly welcome. Get up or get up and be deleted."

Curious about this second commanding voice but not motivated out of hunger or personal interest there really wasn't a reason to respond. I could care less about the needs of this intruder even if they were talking to me. Quartz waited for a few moments in Earth time and a week in shipping container time. Then as if no space had been allotted the word started to drop like cold air from a ceiling vent. "Yes, little container soul of the universe you have been through a great ordeal. Funny enough I would let you go through an extended amount more but that's not up to me and you don't want to wait very much longer. This contraption you called home for a few million years is about to be recycled and that includes you." Quartz provided little in return to the otherwise perfect threat of becoming a recycled soul that would never or could never be the person they were designed to be.

"Look," said Quartz, "if you don't stand up right now then you and only you leave me no choice but to stick this orange sticker on your box. Do you know what the sticker says? No, probably not because you're in a box and I'm holding the sticker and had to take an online class to be orange sticker certified but it says in bold lettering **recycle**. That means it's over pal, the stars will no longer shine on your destiny and the worst part of all is that it will create more paperwork for all of Those that are stuck working in Earth's Shipping Yard.

Please, just stand up and say something, say that you want it to end, say you actually don't like sushi as much as you all tell your friends, sing a song or just stand up and stare at me. Do something human that's reportable as cognitively salvageable. All you have to do is stand and you might see your wife again."

How did Quartz know my wife or care so much that I stood in effort that there was some part of familiar fighting to survive this nightmare and land magnificently at home in bed. A tiny parcel tucked under my heart like an old wedding cake in the back of a freezer. Impossible, it's been too much time. She would have been dead for a millennium. Then again, I'm in a shipping container about to be recycled by thing named Quartz.

"Okay, I'll stand." With no effort the body unfolded into the vertical position. Here you go Quartz, the primordial launch onto two feet that proves our animalistic superiority.

"It speaks," yelled the second voice from above that called itself The Voice and then quickly demanded that I, "Sit down."

"Oh shut up Rodney, you've tortured this one long enough. Go yell at some of the newer shipments. Sorry about that," said Quartz, "but he only knows a few lines, stand up and sit down. Believe it or not that's all he wants to or cares to learn. Anyway you're standing now and there are words to be had between us. There is a lot tossed around about why you are in a forever shipping container, why I'm talking to you and what could happen if we get this conversation correct the first life around. That being said you might want to sit down for this, haha that was a joke. Do whatever makes you feel more prepared to learn as a responsive environment."

With that Quartz popped the orange sticker in his pocket and descended into the container farther to align all four eyes. Two from him and two from the human in the entrapment. At first there was nothing to say, as silence was the only correct action. There had only been memories for so long. Small clips of yesteryears that lacked texture and they were transparent in nature.

Quartz was solid, with a breath that slightly moved the whiskers on my face. I didn't know if I should hug this being or try to sleep with it. Deprivation is cruel to the senses more so than isolation. One is a choice while the other is imprisonment that teased rather than gave reason. "It's okay," said Quartz, "We are going to work through this moment and all the other uncomfortable moments together, you're not at the end but the beginning of life. Still, before we can continue I must read this disclaimer to you. Corporate thinks it's for your own good and let's face it, they're listening."

Welcome to the Earth's Shipping Yard rehabilitation program. In this course, you will learn the important steps that you will need to know before returning to Earth as a better candidate for success. The core should take you around 20 years to complete. If you need to stop at any moment you can't and will just be recycled. Each lesson is to prepare you for a better understanding of the following topics: recycling, volunteering, sexual harassment, and time management. By completion of this course you will understand the importance and functionality of all four topics. Please sign and date at the bottom of the page.

Looking up at Quartz just standing there smiling as They reached forward with the form in one hand and a pen in the other.

There came the overwhelming realization that I didn't really have a choice, the paperwork was signed and with a flick of the wrist it disappeared.

With that Quartz continued, "Okay, with that unpleasant document out of the way we can now divulge in the true gossip pertaining to your situation and how to improve your projected outcome. Losing the smile in trade of fear this overly wise jolly tour guide became stoic. We have to talk about the most important reason why you are here and exactly where here is." A snapping of the fingers cleared the fog in the shipping container to reveal the true surroundings.

"We are in Earth's Shipping Yard. Unlike other shipping yards that move material objects from Coast-to-Coast this particular port deals with rejected souls from the Green Earth Initiative. This was a program in place to help combat the extinction of the planet and everything on board. You are dead and have been rejected by GEI on the grounds that you didn't recycle, drove a gas car and never planted a tree in your life. In fact it's on your final report that you cut down all the trees around your home so you didn't have to rake the leaves. The worst part being the amount of plastic bottles you used in the 38 years you were on the planet. According to the PBA or Plastic Bottle Auditors you used the total of 4865 bottles.

With all that aside, you also flushed four goldfish alongside your pharmaceuticals down the toilet. Your wife on the other hand passed the GEI review. We'll get into that and where she is later. So, what is Earth's Shipping Yard and how do you get a chance to leave here? This containment facility was designed to hold everyone who has been rejected by the GEI until the moment they are freed by their soul mate or are recycled into the processing plant and made into a new soul.

You see, everyone on Earth has a soul mate, this person could be a lover, friend, parent or complete stranger. No matter the situation we are all paired with another soul. As a checks and balances sort of deal they look after you and you were supposed to look after them. The goal is to give both of you the opportunity to live in peace forever in a third dimension described by humans as Heaven. The catch being it must be both of you.

Unfortunately the majority of the time, only one of you meets the requirements set forth by the GEI. In this case you fell into that scenario. You died and were sent to Earth's Shipping Yard to wait for your soul mate to die, in this case your wife. When your wife died she had the option to save you from this container or go back to Earth. This time, along with all the other times, your wife decided to not save you. She would die, see you sitting here and then go back on living without you.

Right now in fact she's living on Earth as if you never existed. To be fair women have taken control of everything by redefining racism and sexism. You're not alone in this scenario but honestly soul mates seem to rarely want to rescue their other half. Probably because in order to do so they have to take on the responsibility of changing your ways. In this story between you and your wife for example she would have had to reform your attitude for being green and leaving a smaller carbon footprint. Yes, chasing Hayden around the room with a can of spray paint was cute but it wasn't carbon friendly. Every time from there on out she would have to get both of you to pass the GEI standards or both of you would return until the decision was made to recycle you both upon death. Hayden as many others just realized it's easier to go on without their other half.

Yes, they face being alone but as long as they go back to Earth they're improving the beauty there and on that rock there are plenty of non soul mate companions.

Look outside, there are so many boxes containing all walks of life that just didn't get it right. That's why I developed the Second Chance Program or Shipping Yard Rehabilitation Program. We had to figure out how to rescue as well as recycle souls.

Using a special birthmark on your skin we are able to tell what we can reuse you for. A triangle with the number one means you can't be recycled, a triangle with the number two means you can only be recycled with the plastics, a triangle with three means you can only be recycled with the metals. Haha, again just a joke. All there really is to go by are the small actions you took on Earth, like saving bugs or turtles from the road. That's where you come in. No matter how much you lived for yourself you always let flies go free from your home. We watched countless hours of you running all around with a plastic Tupperware container trying to catch and release flies. Granted you did give up a few times in on-the-fly survival but overall you are impressive.

That being said you've been given a second opportunity to go back to Earth, find your soul mate and come back together as GEI approved humans. Please do note that you will not be going back to figure out your religion but to save each other from being contributing polluters. Work with a green foot and a light step and eternal peace is yours. If you don't succeed you'll have to try again or be recycled. All depends on your performance. So, do I stick an orange sticker on the side of this unit or are you willing to stand up?

In haste the questions shaped my reality. Why would I fall to Earth in an effort to join a person that had left me not only once but for countless generations? Why save a soul mate that didn't care to save me? And to top all of it off, she, Hayden could see me sitting, standing, sitting, standing in the box and do nothing? The love of my life did nothing and I'm supposed to go crawling back to this place that tossed me out and stored me away from fear that I would only destroy the world without a soul mate? I was out but not without my reason that this is all ludicrous to the point it's maddening.

What nerve the GEI had to discipline me this way, on the basis that I'm not in heaven not because of my spiritual doing but because the Earth was mad about a few trees? I went to church and I gave 10% and all the rest of those requirements and still I was caged like a criminal. Worse, an outcast of the very humanity that ran through my veins and into the streets in an unsung hero kind of way, that only effort to get approval by God so Heaven could save me from Earth only to be asked if I'm willing to go back.

All this time spent waiting has been cruel but not vile and certainly not vicious. Sick with confusion I ask, how much time would be allotted to do this task? Quartz replied, "Let's see you saved 209 flies and on average they live for 28 days, so you will have 14 and 1/2 days on

42

Earth to find Hayden, be green and come back to the GEI for review."

"If Hayden is so great why do I have to go back? Won't she just finish another cycle, see me suffering and go on her merry way? Obviously she doesn't need me or she would have rescued me by now rather than left me in a shipping container."

Quartz, "Oh yes, but this time she is hurting Mother Nature. Another reason you have been given a second chance. Go, save a long time hero from everything you have experienced at Earth's Shipping Yard. Remember, this can only fully conclude when you two make it past the GEI. Don't go back and she'll be placed in a box and you will be recycled. At that point all Hayden will have to do is stand up, sit down and then be recycled because you will have been nothing more than a soda can, repurposed into bicycle parts. From there, if you're lucky you'll get to rust away with each other in a landfill. So, you may as well go back to save Hayden and what's left of the world that needs more soul mates if we are ever going to shut down Earth's Shipping Yard."

In reality, the idea was not to save mankind but to rescue the one person I was placed on Earth to look over but failed to do so. Or did I? Maybe my lack of care made her care more? If we both gave a little would this have just been a situation of two lost souls and a shipping container? There's just too much time to rehash the bad by risking the chance to forget forever. It wasn't Heaven but tempting. It's hard to say what Hayden would be like in a completely different time from my own.

She apparently had an Olympic run on life's stage. We simply group harder experiences that explain themselves through courage as advancements in technology. When I roamed the Earth as a man we had disease and video game units that required controls. Sugar was cheap while pot illegal. Now, what would there be that I would be unprepared for?

By loose estimate it's now been thousands of years if not less but certainly more. So you could fairly say fear was the first restriction on a fast yes. Was my animosity towards the notion of picking up slack where marriage vows had once promised there wouldn't be loneliness? That's the more prompt snag in all of this tassel. How do I get over my torture to ensure a person who would rather let me rot escape the very scenario that they left me in? What hurdles had formed across the line in effort to eagerly laugh in a heart that Hayden clearly did not belong to?

Smoke and mirrors are fun when there's magic, otherwise it's called deceit and not pleasant for anyone trying to explain to their conscience the declaration of a soul mate. Who assigned us to be together anyway? Who had this hidden power that included matching soul mates? All questions that flash directly at the end of Quartz's sentence about being a tool to help close this fictitious Shipyard that was clearly not on Earth. If all it took was to save Hayden to save our planet wouldn't they send more people? Not only that but if the fate of humanity really depended on a person it's all over anyway. Again the questions piled up on the resting shoulders of an imprisoned parcel stuck in a Tupperware container talking to a vacation planner about requiring a wife in a world that was not my own or hadn't been for a few thousand lovers.

"This is rather a big task that you are asked of as a prisoner that is just about to be deleted. Not to mention in a quirky way it lets everything questionable you have done become a misdemeanor of trespassing but still a most definite crime."

"I will admit at this point there is little worth saving in this body that holds no muscle mass or memory of fast food that wants fuel one day into being considered valued. Yet, you are asking me to do the one thing that you can't do and I failed to do. Save Hayden. Save her from what? Did you wipe the smog off the shower glass and realize you failed? Why this person, who has done so well for Earth, so far that my shipping container, is now at the end of the internal loading dock? Who are you really worried about Quartz? What is really in trouble here? You might have orange forms of rejection but the one thing you'll never have is instinct, clarity of emotion when something or an idea is not being completely transparent and you know better.

Tell me Quartz, why do we have to save Hayden? What is really going on the ground that can't be controlled? And Quartz, this is where you need to stand up or sit down but don't be silent because that would only indicate you're not functional. Do you have any extras of those orange stickers?"

Quartz floated a little higher in the room with the direct focus of expanding his position in the order in the container. This had not been a personal cause for an employee of the Earth's Shipping Yard to embellish on as if it was not a free cause that worked out of being fluid. After all, this was not an issue of me or I but us, them, we and in the end ours. Mars was never really a safe haven for humans. Just like all the other trillionaire ideas, space travel was a way to get the population off the Earth so they could extract the resources without the hassle of green riots. Unfortunately, the common person doesn't understand that hostile takeovers are not as fast as an alien invasion alongside an impeachment or the change in the law and even the government issued grant process.

Those who want our trees, oil, and water, we have nothing but time as we are pressed to things. All we have as workers is to escape. Colonizing Mars was not an effort to save the population but an effort to clear the land of indigenous people. Blankets of polio or rockets to another rock, we the people never saw it coming.

Quartz knew how to single out a person in one container through thought and the feelings of being so alone and angry. We had all been tossed through a life not agreed upon that was dictated by those we did not agree with. None of that mattered. Quartz had a job to do as I had a position in the new world. He had to go back and corrupt Hayden. Break her wasteful ways and return her to being peaceful property of the greater good. If I didn't return the buffalo would be shot from trains and hurdled over cliffs.

Yes, we were preparing to leave but the decision was not ours and it should have been. Our blue rock finally started to turn around through the utilization of farmers markets that began to spread like wildfire in 2017. By the time I would go back it would be 3030. Time and space does not exist so why would it matter anyway. Let's just say it's been long enough not to recognize farmers markets. Yes, time has changed but there's never been a lack of heroes. Those willing to stand for what belongs to all of humanity. The select few can never leave our home in trade for the red rock that might have water. Quartz knew better about the images of social media promising water on Mars, he knew better about satellite images of faraway sanctuaries that could be reached by rockets built by technology companies in Napa Valley. He knew that he really didn't have a sex but liked being male. He knew a lot, that wouldn't matter much if I had never stood up in an effort to save Hayden.

At the end of this mind trip there are only a few points worth booking in a mark. If we left the world it would be completely depleted of resources. The majority of us would never make it to Mars and if they did it wouldn't be long that they didn't live. I had to go back and find Hayden. Quartz would help for all three but would settle for the last if nothing was ever successful when greed came into play and in this case even the blue ball was victim to vanity for life. Even if I went back and fell back in love then jumped into a rocket only to expire and have it trailer onto a hostile rotation located deep upon and uninhabitable planet one important point would have been proven.

Soul mates do exist even if the populous group on Earth knew that they're merely a reflection, a shadow that they might not feel alone sitting in the dark. Truthfully, Quartz had just that time in the late 70s when division ruled like it does now. If only there was a Quartz to set a couple straight on the crazy whirlwind that resembles a plastic toy on a track glued to a plastic face, maybe those people would have avoided the recycling. Memories by his side next to old laundry, the battle still had not been pushed far enough to convince the body to just stand up. Quartz could host the children or guilt the desire to repent or rebuke any form of relationship with either kin or get bats out of the ultimate drain and drown any watertight argument. Said, this situation sauntering hard before buoyance kicks in to float their survival.

At this point Quartz and I happened to be talking, dreaming or contemplating for another 20 years or so following Earth's time and all those unrealistic expectations. Left to be the only voice in the room, there had to be some sort of follow-up text that tapped the lonely warrior on the shoulder. The words gave cause to dissolve precious time that was guaranteed over question. I went to sit down out of confusion that now ran amok on Quartz's face. If there would ever be a time to get this parcel of a soul out of this environment and into a survival mode it had passed but most importantly delays started now.

"Hayden, remember, plays the violin not the fiddle even though she enjoys whiskey and knows all the country songs. A bit of hope that pulled you from the wreckage and a day later taught you how to use a bank. This is that uplifting moment where the main character finds strength to fight in the world where everyone knows they don't belong. This is your chapter of all that tells us to chase in circles until you figure out it's all connected,"

Quartz paused then drastically lay back in a chair that had just appeared, "Yes. We are both daydreaming now. Only difference is that this is really happening to you. No rush from Humanity as we all arrived one way or the other, rather waiting to descend or complete recycling at the GEI program. Truthfully, I found the wings of an endangered butterfly and then was in random pain by unpredictable weather. In short, who can really tell what you're going to accomplish and who cares? You're just some fool in a marginal shipping container with infinity walls that could or could not win the day and a life back that was squandered in the start."

The great voice rang from above, "Are you drunk? No? We are simply losing time with you." This was the first time either one of them heard the voice say anything other than scripted lines.

Quartz and I had sat and lost time together for a few more years according to Earth's time. There was a sense of urgency in the conversation but this journey could not be rushed if it were ever launched. I needed to gain confidence about myself that this return to life was the right choice and that saving Hayden would be worth the effort to save Humanity. Procrastination's outcomes would result in similar narratives. The first fate would be that I would waste enough time fighting Quartz that the shipping container would reach the end of the yard and simply disappear. Option two, would be that he could fix the past by correcting what will be in the future.

"Quartz, why do you care so much about my case? What has brought on the volume of your pretense in this descending moment? Are there not millions if not billions of others that would jump on the chance to return? I have everyone's greedy reward as my own but the freedom to live the way I'm ultimately going to live? You are a kind keeper of the containers but your selflessness reminds me of a sales agent that only wants to access my credit. This talk about redemption with the return and heroism sticks to the buyer's remorse. Only difference here is I don't want to be given a receipt. No, this is all sales, a final sort of deal and I'm just not buying the store closing.

Tell me how can all of humanity go completely bankrupt to the point only the rejected employees can save the company? You fired me remember? Wrote me off, what I had spent my time doing as offensive to the overall benefits. Not a team member but an individual that could repeat the garbage that was expected to be regurgitated at every new face. Do you want to know something? I liked cutting down those trees, burning their limbs that would later be poured into a plastic bag and tossed out. Revenge comes to point when the feeling of your punishment sings send. What if I don't spend my days fixing my ex but instead I fill them with purchases and chainsaws? Just because we seem to have the same

DNA does not mean my intentions would be favorable to all of us. What tools have many of times turned on their living counterparts still standing, the same way they used to before being carved up after selection. Quartz, how do I know that you are not cutting me down only to shape me as a tool of destruction instead of a bolt that will hold the unifying bridge between extinction and hope?"

"Call me out as you may but your few words have a distance that leaves room for carelessness and doubt. We have spent years now arguing about the what ifs and Earth as far as I can tell you're spending too much time delivering words about diversity to me."

"If everything is okay, can't this wait for another few thousand years?"

"Your behavior is rather monotonous for the end of times being on the back of the next sunset."

"Fictional as you may be, there's not enough trust in your requests that could pass as reasonable. That's why I decided to make my internal peace with what has been done and what will be done and whatever man crawls out of the sea. Quartz, I wish you luck but it's time for us to say goodbye. There's a promised recycle day coming to alleviate my fictitious pain and that's an idea well welcomed!"

Quartz rapidly relied, "You selfish individual who is blind with pity constructed out of banana leaves! Everything you have said rather starts with I or had I in the mind's eye. Sad as that is we still feel like there's hope in a relic. Time has gone its merry way here, the world has a day to fight for more time to kill, ponder, ravage, converse, learn, disqualify and worst of all think over the simplicity of everything.

It was only at the moment when breathing took a password that there was a revelation. You will not be returning to a dystopia. No, you will in fact be arriving in Utopia. After you died, there was a movement of young protesters that failed to see the value of stuff over the environment. They were equipped with time due to the lack of a good-paying job mixed with the explosively high cost of education. Those still young enough in grade school even weaponized the use of their free-thinking parents as the use of impressing our kids so we can work transitioned out. So did a lot of the distraction from what was really going on.

Not to mention every person on Earth was entitled with a communication device that transformed the time it took to reach other like-minded Rebels. It was only a matter of time before the blue bubble popped and people took to the streets to peacefully ask the politicians nicely in a harsh tone to please do something about the state of global warming. A young girl on the autism spectrum leaving rise to be the next generation's leader in the green movement. For once, it and all of it looks to have been resolved by the ever-growing demand to lower carbon to the knees of the outspoken.

Words would not justify the excitement that came over Earth's Shipping Yard during all of this time. For the first second in a thousand years it appeared that the shipping yard would have to be closed. There would no longer be a need for souls to go back and change what they had done. People were going to all pass right through the GEI standards. Earth would be the brightest white and green that modern occupants had ever seen. Cancer would dissipate alongside most diseases. Obesity and hunger would be buried in the same grave. Utopia came to light without the use of oil.

Then, just as the quality for all of life emerged it was beheaded by those not willing to lose control of the light. And now, bullied fossil fuel companies made their last move. By the time most of society knew what had happened the collateral damage was burning away faster than ever before while the shipping yard grew a thousand times it's designed size.

The national anthem is played on what was left of the radio station. Journalism went extinct with the loss of common electricity and food was available in cans for those willing to enlist. A few Rogue writers like Word Revolt distributed illegal pamphlets until their paper warriors were assassinated when delivering to the last of the lending libraries. In turn, all libraries and collections of books became a federal offense.

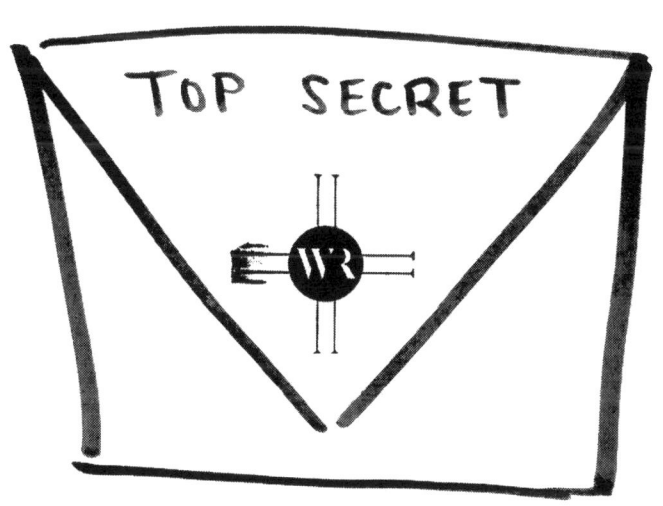

Guns and any reading material were contraband and required to be forfeited over to the government of that region. Art was the last to go but just like the prohibition there were areas of underground bands of artists that held secret shows on the third Thursday of every month. The laughter had all but stopped only to be replaced with dietary elbows. The population was once again fighting for survival let alone doing well enough to care about the trees.

In war, every nation sucks in their ability to launch the most destructive form of flight that aims to land on those who repress them the most. In a matter of weeks the years of accomplishments were lost. As it always is, the best way to win over an enemy is to delete their culture. Churches, mosques, art schools, museums and libraries were all recycled to rubble. Data centers along with hard drive farms that contained the cloud were the second locations to be unplugged. Knowledge was now left distinctly in those who had retained the information internally. Even the majority of those people fell victim to what we know as the cleansing. Nothing was left in the end but a few survivors pushing the working class into bloody outcomes.

Cancer would have come back only to make friends with lung disease which brutally held the hand of Earth's children while leading us into a busy street of drunk drivers. Protesters would have been recorded from earlier years only to be assigned the front lines that would never hold. Slowly, over a short time the population dwindled with the exhaustion of supplies. Resources of mass destruction went extinct in the same fashion as rations.

Comfort shined in the glow of another crater on a traditionally smooth street. The fight began with fire only to be met by morning. We had destroyed our accomplishments as humans. What made us cry or think had all been removed from the daily grind. There were no more theatrical plays or musicians performing in outlandish costumes at football games. We couldn't even take our dog for a walk around the block because the majority of families had to eat them. People tried to eat cats too but they tasted too much like judgment.

Before the last explosive interruption fell from the gray storm cloud, the people of the world agreed on a ceasefire. The target was successfully hit, killing the last of the newborns in the United States. There would have been a candlelit remembrance but no one remembered how to make candles. Parents were just left standing upon the rubble at the end of their creation. At this moment there had been enough loss to break every survivor into believing war could not be the solution. Bullies had always held unfavorable dislike but somehow war was different. Battles had to be fought for freedom to be able to shop at Walmart.

There had to be conflicts in other parts of the world that ensured prices would remain low. Proud to be an American meant we would do anything to preserve our standard of capitalism that had to be cheap in order for there to be a well-functioning country. It didn't matter what lens had to be polluted in order to keep our way of life available to everyone. Those staples being, Internet, water, food like substances and sex. For those four needs we destroyed the structure of society while freeing our minds from all the technology that was so close to giving time not to be wasted.

Everyone was murdered just shortly after the mainstream use of electric cars joined the Internet. Yeah, it was all that would be blamed. None of this would matter when the tears finally stopped falling. Red eyes took the appropriate time to clear in effort to see what had happened. Where did all this go awry? Ninety percent of the hearts on Earth had now made a pilgrimage to The Shipping Yard.

Years would have to pass before the remaining leader starved in the standard underground bunkers. Decades more would have to pass before high blood pressure would kill the remaining elders. Eventually, what was left were a group of young adults that had grown up in despair but had the freedom to blossom.

Just as a weed can emerge from the blacktop a new generation broke free from the hardened surface that covered them. Deep down the soil was still rich enough to produce survivors. Especially, now that culture had been reduced to soil. That dirty Earth we all avoided would now be the life form needed to give rise to our needs. Pollution left little ground that still held the nutrients willing to produce a crop. Entire parking lots were stripped of the pavement to find clean ground to start anew. Oddly enough, the more soiled it was the better protected it had been under layers of poured foundations.

To free our individual needs there was a call to band together in an effort to consolidate the talent that remained. Now that the war was long over and people had the basics covered. Food, shelter, safety, and sex it was time to reconsider how to go about establishing government. For that to happen there needed to be a form of communication. All of the power grids have been destroyed along with any wires that connected two states let alone multiple countries.

That's when the horse had its revival. The Pony Express was re-animated. Very slowly, letters were attached to brave carriers that held the unique responsibly of traveling state to state delivering the mail that was now recognized. From the States, sailors would carry parcels to other carriers, branching to all the major ports across the world in an archaic practice as a letter would now take months rather than seconds but served as an effective starting point.

You should have seen the mail ships. Equipped with gardens that produced vegetables off the bridge of the boat and chickens that not only provided meat but in their eggs a sense of direction. Yes, humanity had survived in an abundant way that if anything held meaning in every conversation. We couldn't text, email and most definitely not ignore our fellow survivors.

More so out of the fact that we did not want to. Every person on the ground now had value. They were worth the knowledge they retained no matter the subject, every bit of the trade held the same importance as the one presented before it. Music held arms with engineering, as did math with poetry. Finally we the people including all the people of the planted had one goal in mind. To rebuild a society that was cleaner, happier, more understanding and definitely did not waste resources on items that could be used to threaten others to do our bidding.

Pleasure belonging in the clouds and not in our hearts or actions, we ate together or we worked together to eat. There was not time to be a king. From the Pony Express particular birds were taught to deliver small messages just like the carrier pigeons. Except now Parrots and Hawks were used depending on the season or region. From thoughtfulness, technology crawled back from the tar pits in California, this time we did not focus on stuff. This time companies were only given permits to form if they were trying to fix the damages from the war, provide food or figure out how to reverse pollution.

Again, the pendulum has swung while the Earth's Shipping Yard went into the black then the red. Utopia once again was forming out of necessity driven change, powering the collective performers to focus on the now. What was left was little but luckily those left remaining were just as scarce. No one cared though because the standard of life went up. Yes, there were no longer bars or Internet but the drinks that existed had heart while the clothing was handmade by a person that loved you or needed you in their circle of craftspeople.

EARTH

Money had all disappeared and with it were the politics and constructs that fulfilled a lot of the issues that reigned over us before the war. After all, if an issue is not popularized is it really an issue or political campaign aiming to draw lines? There could never be a winner before the bombs dropped because to have an opponent means you must disagree enough to win. In winning there is power, the human mind will do anything it can to maintain the status of authority.

It's crazy how far the idea of being correct has tossed the possibility of Utopias off its proven course. Humility is a taught weakness that we simply can't do well while promoting political agendas. Wavering would cause the position of knowing everything. Thankfully, all of that was now as important as trash day. The very factories that bred the need for recycling, trash pickup and large debris removal had all been eliminated.

That exhaustion was also large for corporations funding political candidates. With no commercials mixed with the death of mass communication the only way to reach a voter was by snail mail. Wood was once again carved to make printing easier while old tires were also carved and ran on wood stoves to mass-produce marketing material.

Ha, the once silent hum of dreadful white noise had ended while industry passed a small ember of hot hope in effort to enact the fire that would be the only flame in history to bring peace. You see, this flame was not forged from industry or stuff but rather the inventive Spirit of living well with the Earth. Long chapters have been written about the removal of resources. Yet, no one has ever written about how we plan on replacing them.

Instead of the alchemy of making gold we should have been focused on the renewal of what's been sucked from the middle. Think about it, what happens if we continue to take from the core of our planet and destroy its weight by turning it into a gas? Eventually the gas that is on top powers the ground we walk on. Out of that an exact thought was born, the GEI. Everyone on Earth is free to pass through unless their balance of materials being delivered into the sky outweighs their balance of materials on the Earth.

In this case it's an amount versus population ratio. If more weight is being mined in the ground than the population can absorb from the sky an alarm is triggered. As in everything in life, there needs to be a balance in the give-and-take. Even though we are in Utopia and stable right now, your soul mate is polluting more than what her share should be. That's why you are not recycled. While your wife has been okay, she has not been great. Your stay at the Earth's Shipping Yard has really been insurance if not anything else. Through our statistics software you to have been red flagged as dangerous to sustainability. While you have been convicted guilty, outside of the courts you soul mate has had the opportunity of being an offender and it is a matter of threat to the GEI."

Quartz, took a second as the chair based in satin is transformed from a patio seat into a recliner. The shape of their body also androgenized. Clearly preparing to handle all views that might be brought up solely out of looks.

Quartz continued, "Hayden, early last year became a follower of the ambient practices of the past. Learning how to grow tobacco while seeking out chemical compounds that bind pigments together in an effort to produce long-forgotten paint. GEI says she even broke food grade eggs to use in her creations. The berries she collects to make ink are not currently protected, we must think of the birds. Hayden is wasting Earth's supplies to produce art and that simply does not follow the needs of humanity. After the banning of cadmium yellow, we took to the process of eliminating all unuseful practices like this but not exclusive to art. Spinach does not need to be ground up for the green color just as mustard should not be abused for the yellow.

On top of all this, Hayden has turned to hunting for her food and then uses the hides to paint on instead of producing clothing or shelter. If Utopia is going to survive the industrial use of materials must be used in effort to better everyone as a whole. Creation has its limits and those limits are keeping those left in Paradise alive as well as being a top-grade custodian of what's left of the planet.

Waste is not an option or gift, it's a valued resource that will not be ignored. Also, unfortunately, her action that is ultimately why we have decided to send you, is the fact that Hayden has resurrected tobacco. Currently she is using this toxin to make a small batch of cigarettes that she calls, *Little Betsy's*. After they insanely grow in popularity a businesswoman monopolizes the product to the world. Particular people would like to monetize on the effects of this seemingly harmless back yard hobby that has the possibility to endanger the Utopia and world that now exists.

All we need from you is to go back and become a chain smoker in 14 days, to dissuade her from sharing the recipe. With your history this should only take a few days after you convince her to love you. If you fail there will be violence that leads to weaponization. Trust me when the words are as clear as the following. You are not alone. It didn't ail the Shipping Yards that you are singled out in this mission. No one knows how to stop Hayden like you do. You can diverge her path or translate an alternative choice.

If Hayden takes Utopia and gives it to manufacturing then we are all going to be at the shipping yard for very long time. Currently, the world is learning the cello while the dictionary is being pieced together with some fragments found all over the globe. If it's at any moment we need to curtail negative influence it is now. Earth has clear-minded constraints, janitors if you must, that love the rock tossing harmlessly through space for the first time since the cavemen.

Is it not worth going back to preserve the few who never had the opportunity to meet addiction? Think about it, this tobacco would be the first drug to be reintroduced into human hands after thousands of years. Hayden, out of her innate displacement to make art will tarnish everything the war was about. Cleansing the planet of all the wrong and redoing civilization from a fresh beginning.

You and I have an opportunity to rewrite the discovery of everything that led up to the last fight. Let's fix this by muting the malleable before anything can take shape. Prohibition forced people while we are giving the

66

masses what they have already asked for. Save them from addiction and trashing the planet and to leave a civilization that holds balance above all.

Hayden, has an Earthly experience that withdraws when it comes to death or greater understanding. You can alter that. Make her see that it is not about the lifespan of a human but the existence of a species. Rather we came from swamps or God we are all here fighting to survive to appease a belief that there must be something more than Earth. Science does its job to make everything look as small or as large as it once was but dreams turn imagination into magic that in turn allows energy to do as it will on our bodies. If something greater did exist we would never lose a loved one but on the other hand who deploys the random?

I'm not here to convince you about religion, as that seems to have all the convincing it needs. Especially, to those who are currently raising a generation of churches as we speak. No, we are having this conversation on the grounds of a steel floor floating its way to an end. Innovation is what brought the shipping yard to accept popularity and innovation is what will shut this atrocity down.

Go back, tell Hayden of the looming disaster of her recreation and save what is the longest period of peace Earth has ever felt. Otherwise we are all going to be stuck as guidance counselors in a school full of potential threats. Change history and clear Humanity's title from being the only monster fiction can't predict. Your shoulders are thin but that's what pads and misdirection are for. It's simple, all you have to do is hold your hand to your heart."

Quartz once again transformed from an androgynous shape to a male then to a female and the chair changed according to the beliefs. Propaganda had not gone away in the stars that now held those afloat captive in small rectangular moments constructed of corrugated steel. Dissension of time is now upon the duo while neither cared for the other representative.

After all, after death who cares for Earth and in death who cares for the Shipping Yards? "Okay, Quartz. Where are you sending me and what do I need to know?

Quartz had little intention on bouncing on the opportunity to prosper over the decade-long argument that was held between worker and the incarcerated. Truthfully, the win meant an end to the easy material from the pamphlet withdrawn from the book. Except this book was hard to write, not to mention the complexity of explaining the plot. They were no longer free sections of waste that could be allotted for such preparedness as liquid between the fluff and the facts had become tired and short. Just as a passenger learning to use a cocktail napkin as a parachute while the hot air sips ducks out of the atmosphere. The ultimate free fall had begun, a descent from the top to deletion. If I did not leave by the end of this thought or a week in Earth's time there'd be no part for me to lean on.

The shipping container would cross the yellow line at the end of the yard and as it came would go. Recycled to the point there would be a concept like glass or aluminum but not the soul. In many ways Quartz had thought to just let this one be. Others slipped away for management so why not this one. It really is unfair to ask about what is being demanded. We all come to that depressed epiphany, looking to swoon our passions into walking the line of shame and a memory of fame.

Black cars alone, it's simpler to just let go of a reason in effort to forge new cars in the morning. At least then the coffee will be fresh and the story new if not different. Maybe, just maybe, I should be free from the burden provided the chance to visit Earth more times than anyone in the Shipping Yard.

Yes, if this fails my soul mate and I will be charged to go through the process once again, or sentenced to another seven thousand years by the partner who will revive the full term of 100,000 years or until the end of Earth. But in that there may be a great pause of a particular moment resting in luxury, left for those already recycled or still on Earth running their first lap around the Sun. A revolution, now to conclude with action that went up or down but not parallel like it had gone on for this long.

With Quartz backed against the wall, three deep breaths took too long to resurrect. All that was left was to find a way to regurgitate the circumstances on the blue rock while seeming hopeful that this recreation would be successful for everyone. All Quartz had to start with was the quote his grandmother said before she was recycled out of stubbornness, "Too much butter is not bad." Dying of heart failure at 90 would simply prove the effectiveness of the quote.

Earth, as it is right now can only be described as euphoric. Paradise for those willing to be kind while studying the gift that is our rock. Trees are planted daily,

70

flowers grow in a community garden that was once a gas station. Food is grown with love to only be digested with respect. The majority of the grogginess looming in the sky is now cleared. People walk around as people instead of folks holstering opinions. TV and the radio had long been muzzled with classical music. Granted classical music is and was political to the lack of words to help bring less distraction from meditation or other green workshops.

The populace was at once free enough to push the boundaries of being alive. Just like the great pendulum swing of 2030 when polluting the world became a war crime, and everything was acceptable. So acceptable that those willing to experiment to further a study would bring back trickier practices that funded free pollution just like in the beginning.

Chapter Three. Part I

Once the overwhelming guilt of not going to Earth made blood feel like mud, bones became anxious with the final decision to return the Earth. The people had to be stopped from returning to the very vices that polluted the mind and soul in the early years. Even at this moment tobacco barns are being raised in secret to grow leaves for the production of cigarettes. Bottles of every kind ran down an assembly line to later be filled with water or other single-use drinks.

A little mess became the symbol of award for those remaining on the pristine planet. Gold star stickers along with glitter once again found refuge in the ocean. The first fish in over a thousand years died from eating trash left behind by a candy bar. As a whole the blue sphere looked healthy but in the veins of the matter the flu had already started attacking the healthy blood cells.

It was only a matter of time before carbon would be reborn into its formal monster. Being selfless in this selfish Renaissance was not going to be easy but almost impossible. Out of those left on Earth who would be old enough to remember what our stuff once did to the environment? Why would people change their ways amongst everything looking so great? Who would be able to set aside leisure in trade for long days of painful work? Was this saving of the Earth not worth this generation giving up a perceived Utopianism?

Time lingered by the constraints of this mission weighing heavy out of doubt and defeat. In observance to the silence Quartz appeared with the cool wind flowing around arrival. This is going to be a challenge for sure but if you don't go the challenges will only grow to outnumber the odds.

There's a time limit to this conversation that will expire faster than an Earthling growing up. At least try to help instead of moping about what has not already won you over. Challenge the cause on an even emotional battlefield, not one where you start at the bottom of the hill sweating and in tears. Stand up for a Utopian Earth that is already in place but just needs a little redirection. Hayden will listen to you if you arrive a winner, not the slob or pushover you were last time. Sharing a glance for a moment long enough to produce 1000 more plastic parts slipping past the two thieves.

Quartz, stretching out long decorative arms, clears his imaginary throat and leans into a few more words. Another reason you have to go soon is that if you don't a company out of the last war will start producing guns for recreational target use. If and when they do there will be no stopping another age of sludge. Power over others will slip back into fashion and well, the one percent will take what they wish and everyone else will go back to working for a set wage.

It will all start when one Beringer brother accidentally shoots the other in the yard when they are fighting over the last cigarette. In turn the brother that was shot would go on to live but later killed his brother to gain control of the company. Armies are sooner born and from there we're all back to daydreaming about living on Mars. Earth's Shipping Yard will grow ten times the size it is now and everyone who's already here who will be erased to make room.

Including you your great-grandchild and great-great-grandchild. Unfortunately, those two took after you and all matters of living green. "Stand up," echoed the long absent voice. Quartz, a little weary replied, "it's time to stand up and get going or the moment to send you back will be too late and you'll never have enough time. All of that aside there was still a soccer team that needed to breathe fresh air the way it was intended for the lungs. You might be the support Earth's Shipping Yard needs for there to be a tomorrow of planting a seed where it is dropped.

Chapter Three. Part II

"Okay, what needs to be done for this trip back to Mother Earth?" Quartz being overjoyed clapped whimsically while all the air turned warm with relief, "There's not much to do really but for you to close your eyes and say Hayden. That's it."

"That's all there is to bring me out from the dead? To free me from the shipping container ran by a fish person and his bully friend The Voice? There must be more! What year will it be, will I resemble the old me or will the body be someone else? At least tell me what country this will take part in." Quartz smiled while turning from a young fish into a representation of Hayden, "Take my hand, close your eyes, say my name." I did just that in almost a mocking fashion. Then a voice as clear as a spring rain carried out through the air with the smell of fresh-baked bread, "Sorry, do we know each other?" Opening one eye, I was standing there behind Hayden in line at a bakery on Earth.

There the two of us stood staring at one another wanting to buy bread at Kim's Bakery. Sun wrapped over our skin while noises of all sorts fought to rip the attention of the moment apart. Sweet aromas danced peacefully around our chests matched with sour wafts of coffee that passed right through the air. Little ones giggled under tall ones anticipating their selection from the chalkboard above the counter. Coffee beans crashed like romantic lovers until there is no separation to be had. This moment cannot be fought but only enjoyed with a little butter or cream cheese. A teenager walks by with a cup of what had to be pure vanilla brought to life by caffeinated sugars. All of this pleasure gliding around the person in front asking a simple question that could never be answered in such a short euphoric line.

Quickly it became Hayden's turn and out of the flow of the room she returned to place an order completely forgetting about if she knew me or not. She staggered to wait for her order on the left side of the counter while a blonde little girl with the cheer of fresh snowflakes asked for my order.

"May you have everything a person alive in the morning hours can possibly want," she said.

Bagels, cakes, pastries all mixed with smoothie juices and coffee. What would be first to touch my tongue after so long being stuck in a shipping container, somewhere between Heaven and Hell? Just then Hayden received her order and turned to walk out the door. There's no time for breakfast after all, falling out of line to chase the mission down the street, around the bend and then she stopped.

Hayden spoke with a certainty that wore kindness as a Sunday dress, "Why are you following me sir?"

With no idea how the face that faced Hayden looked, I knew that caution had to be on display. "Well, you see your friend told me that you made the best cigarettes in town. Was wishing on a switch that you could provide a little?"

Nervous, I new that line sounded a little poetic but it had already left the body's lips. "I do make a fine traditional cigarette stranger but I don't always share with those unknown. Why don't you walk with me to my car and if you have been convincing enough there might be a few drags in your future, if not, you're on your own for a fix."

"Sounds fair." Let's go quickly as time is also important in this scenario. The two walked with a brisk but peaceful manner towards a gray electric car sitting already started a block away. She could have had the car pick her up but this challenge and direction peaked her interest. After all it's not every trip to the coffee exchange that a stranger walks in and deja vu approaches you about a project that was supposed to be a secret. In fact Hayden had only started to experiment with tobacco at this time and only a select group of partners knew about the mischief.

Anyway the both of them had some regurgitation of the truth to distract from the left or right onlooker. "So," Hayden said to break the already long stride, "Who told you about my Little Betsy's? They really are not all that popular as of now or in a few specific months."

"Oh," I said, "just the word around the power grid that you had something special smoking in that lab of yours and that it was the hottest." Hayden laughed and grabbed me by the shoulder to give me reason to stop walking and free the chatter.

"Okay, who are you? What or how much do you know about it? Cigarettes are only a hobby of mine. I don't trade them with anyone. Think of the smoke and I as lovers that only meet in a hotel once a month. Only in this scenario, we are both single and the only issue we are hiding is pollution. What's a little pollution between lovers? A little trash amongst passion? Why is it so wrong for girls to produce a little trash in the sheets? For you? What did you say your name was?"

Silent to the visuals left by the previous questions I thought to use another name other than the one we had both known. "My name is," I'm willing to lie, my old name came out naturally to meet Hayden eyes. We both stood on the solar sidewalk sharing another moment of recollection willing itself to live longer than before. "Well sir, that is a great name but what are your intentions? What are we doing here talking about nonsense? There must be something or somewhere we both have to be at around this time."

With that Hayden turned to walk the rest of the way to her car. All long trying to remember where she heard that name before. She knew this person but from where and more importantly when did she know them from? Paranoid, Hayden took the longest way back to her dwelling in the country where it wasn't until a cup of tea was made and the door locked that safety nestled into her lap. The rest of the night was spent flipping through town registries trying to hunt down the stalker from the café but nothing familiar had arose, as for her entire lifetime that name was not spoken as it was over 1000 years ago.

I had an intrinsic night, proud of luck that mine was the body that was picked for the mission, it was clothed but the clothing did not house a wallet. No form of identification or redeemable cash that in forethought would be extinct. That did not matter, as the first rotation would be spent walking around and marveling at the sleepy land of Greenville.

Everything here was boasting a sense of purpose, designed to help the Earth and not rob from its wonders. All available surfaces were covered in solar panels or disguised as everyday objects. Billboards read positive mantras instead of flashy advertisements while being plugged into street lights that provided a warm glow over purposely placed trees. Buildings made of organic materials cleaned the air while flowers on the rooftops hosted food for bees and butterflies.

Giant was just as absent as flashing signs while sustainable lived at an everyday address. Some stores grew food by means of aquaponics for the community by providing organic essentials like shirts, shoes and sun hats. Color was also a major implement in the town's creation. Bright yellows, purples and even deep Reds and blues died the fabric of the walls instead of masking a surface with paint.

Windows, raw and handmade were full of bubbles that helped to warm the home on cooler nights. Although by the looks of things the windows and doors were never closed. For there was a cool breeze constantly passing over warm air and there wasn't a need for heating air or the fear of safety as everyone was relying on one another to do their part. There was so much more to explore but the town started to yawn and I realized that everyone else had gone to sleep in order to greet the sunrise.

In fashion to the time it was now the moment to ask, where is there to sleep in a perfect system? One road ran on through the streets and out of town then over a few bridges. The idea was to escape from the people. If there were no people around, no one would care where a body would rest. After a few miles carried by feet, exhaustion settled in leaving every option desirable.

Soon, a large tree with a bed of pine straw offered rest for the sense of motherly protection so that it became home. Lying there under the tree in the new time I could not help but wonder if this is how a time traveler would feel. Lost but surrounded by familiarity. Out of place but still resembling a human in form.

Then it hit, it's been two thousand years since my last dream. Would there be a dream or just a pause, then consciousness? Seconds. Most of the night went by awake until there was not enough fear to keep the body wide eyed. The want to sleep came with a tiny voice in the distance so far away that not even a dog with big ears could make out the verbiage. Slowly, the sound rang a little louder, louder, it's still too distant. All except The Voice was dark. Every time The Voice rang out a bright white light rained amongst the vibrations. Louder still but just not there to repair tinnitus all of the timing felt familiar. Like being back in the shipping container.

Hours passed this way with clarity always just a moment too far out of reach. Until it was morning I felt the hours of rest would be haunted by something that would not come forth.

Almost used to the dream the sound with the power of the light rang loud enough to shake the tree. Awake, I repeated what the voice had run through during the hours of peace, "stand up." Even being as far away as Earth there is not enough distance to end the truth about Earth's Shipping Yard.

Now early morning, the sun still low in the sky there was a moment to refocus on the mission, purpose or cause as to why all this was. Slightly distracted by the rejuvenated beauty of the Earth there simply was not time to enjoy a single moment of self indulgence. Hayden had to be stopped in a persuasive way to make her realize why the populace cannot go back to their old ways. Fortunately, the town was small and Hayden loves routine. If there was any truth to her repetitive notions she should be standing in line at the coffee exchange waiting on her drink that was in a cup of native seeds that would later be planted with all the other seed cups on the edge of the forest.

Quickly I became vertical to the horizontal rush for town. Over the bridge and past the fields of amber, through the collection of milkweed until finally arriving in town. The flowers had just started to open on the rooftops making the air smell stronger than a spilled bottle of perfume. Sneezing continuously, a fellow stranger walked by suggesting the consumption of more local honey. There's no time to ask why and I continued hand over foot to the bakery.

Like clockwork Hayden was standing in line upon arrival. Walking up behind her I cleared to the fixed route, "Hayden?" By the way her shoulders tensed there was evidence she knew the voice behind her. Not turning around she's simply ignored the advance. Again, "Haden?" Still, nothing but this time she stuck her hands in the pockets of a hemp dress covered in mountains. One more time, "Haden?"

"Okay, what do you want?" said Hayden turning around. "We have to talk about your little Betsy's. There's something important we must discuss before there are too many people and not enough shipping containers." Lost, Hayden turned back around to focus on her order. "If you do not stop this production of goods bad things are going to happen. This Utopia will end and Earth will find itself back in the 2020s."

Hayden turned her head sideways just enough to where the corner of her eye could be seen, "Stop, we have nothing to talk about." The baker called her to the counter and showed her the same drink as yesterday and she fell to the left side of the counter to wait. I called her again but this time using a more direct approach that caught the eye of the overall peaceful crowd, "Just sit with me for one cup of coffee and if you're still not interested in a few moments this will be over, as if it never happened until what you're being warned about actually happens."

"Fine, one cup." Hayden's order is called and the two walk outside to sit on a park bench across the street away from open ears. Sipping her drink she realizes her counterpart didn't order anything, "Why did you not get a drink? Are you just there for me?"

"No money or trust me, food just might be more tempting than you are." I answered without thinking. "Money?" Hayden looked at me. "Yeah, lost my wallet last night." Or so it seemed. "Wallet?" She said, "What are you talking about Sir?" Quickly realizing that either money or a wallet might not be a thing in this time, I adjusted the response to, "Yes, the only reason for being here is to see you."

"You are a strange one Sir and this half-full cup is wearing so this little meeting is almost over." Panic set in, "Okay Hayden here's the truth." Out of the next hour I explained life, death, Earth's Shipping Yard and what was going to happen if she continued to make little Betsy's. At the end her coffee was long gone, the story told to completion leaving only a haunting pause between Hayden and I looking blankly at the bakery with large sunflowers growing off the roof. Hayden was again the first to speak.

"My little Betsy's kill the world? My organic little Betsy's bring armies back to plunder our resources while killing humanity? Weapons become resurrected out of history and lead to the overpopulation of everything? Little Betsy's raise major manufacturing that causes carbon to heat the air like it did once upon a time? And you are my husband from 2,000 or so years ago that was captured in a shipping container in the sky because I did not rescue you? Only to be freed to stop me from making cigarettes? Sir, that is one fantastic fable. Maybe you should go type it out on a typewriter or better yet write it down in a book."

Laughing, Hayden stood up and turned to me, "Thank you for a wonderful morning eviction but I have Little Betsy's to make." Pulling a cigarette out of her pocket she looks around then tossing the Betsy to me.

"Enjoy, if you want another you'll have to figure out a trade." Walking away there was a growing distance of her two feet. If she would not listen then there is no sense in persistence. There had to be another way to shake pain from her Little Betsy's. Hours past while the flowers on the top of the building started to close one after the other until the roofs all had turned green and been shadowed by night.

® *LITTLE BETSY'S*

Tastes like a first kiss!
In your friend's basement
after a long night
of dancing at prom
* Gaurunteed or half back in coupons

Chapter Four. Part I

Once again the pastel town had started to slow so I went back to the tree a few bridges away. That night was harder as hunger started to set in. Still there's no sense in sleeping if dreaming meant to be stuck listening to that voice. The stars came out as I sat under the tree playing with the cigarette known as a Little Betsy. Paper smelled sweet and the tobacco had a vintage look. It was rolled with no filter but this was just the beginning. I laughed at the idea that floated into the night air but nothing substantial came until a turtle wandered across the moment. The reptile paid no attention to my issues and only cared about eating whatever was growing in the grasses. Looking down at the cigarette I thought about eating it. Then the darkest of ideas came by in a blink.

When was the last time an animal in this town died by pollution? All life came and went in such a natural rhythm that if life were to be stopped by a handmade product there would be chaos. Utopia disrupted but notified. Reaching over I picked up the little turtle that showed no signs of fear as humans have lived with nature in harmony for so long. Time went by with just the two of us staring at each other in wonder of what would happen next. If this little life was ended for the greater good would that be just? How could the death of this little reptile be what is needed and on only the second day.

This resurrection was to save life on Earth, not to add to the pending distraction. Would this be seen as evil and in another blink of the eye this body left while my soul returns to the container? Choices became more difficult than I had remembered. Then again there was never a need to directly kill a small creature. It was much easier to just toss trash away and never think of the consequences again. Is directly killing still a form of human pollution? All this would do is remove the actual need of the middle person known as waste. The deep breath followed by a tear and the little turtle became silent in a warm lap. That night I slept sitting up with a nervous spine pressed against the bark of the elder tree. There had been moments like this alive but not moments like this after killing.

Lying down came to sponsor a feeling of righteousness that battled guilt in the same way the seasons change. At least sitting there was an aspect of work that provided the calming sensation of labor. After all what is a deed that is lazy? No, this assassination had to feel as if it was earned. Even if being alive in a time where I was not a character, there still had to be ownership of action to perform a simple and selfless act that would have never existed the first time around.

Soaking it in that the first time around never required murder's axe. Daft decisions of ignorance lived off of impulse, nutrients capsulated in packaging that fed the body and mind. Ownership of the end result won

90

over comfort of a well-rested night. All there was left to do was to tuck remorse under a bottom lip and figure out how Little Betsy's could be the murder weapon. But for now the thought of burying a cold turtle slipped away from focus while the tired mind gave way to rest.

In this night I would not dream or fantasize about The Voice. Instead there would be silence. Absolute calm of the long dark six hours of sleep. Intoxicated out of natural human chemical not even common sense would feel the sun rise. In fact, the body would lack the care of noon or dinner, sleeping clear through into the next day. Some may argue trauma or the lack of food but the truth is that time just needed to pass. Just enough of the priceless commodity that moves without command.

A perfect Utopian child would find a lone person under a tree with a dead turtle on the lap and a cigarette hanging from a stranger's lips. Yes, moments had to clear the calendar before gaining up on me and the situation under the tree. Fate's Utopian child discovered the situation there and had an entire day to spread the news about what was found just outside of town over a few bridges and perched in a field under a tree.

For too many kind words the entire town had gathered to interview me, sleeping as death rested in a green shell. Before long, detention for those deemed important took breaks from gardening to adventure out into the country. The town had arrived at the hills that have a hidden time traveler. All except one.

Hayden was talking softly in a greenhouse that did not exist, working on the next flavor of Little Betsy's that she called *Strawberry Kiss*. Unannounced to her out of focus, she was the only one in the greenhouse that day. Time caught up in the moment perfectly planned to guide serendipity right on through into the next generation. The moment came to unplug the barrel of marbles with a single sneeze from the youngster that found me, two sets of eyes opened.

Startled, I opened one eye and then the other as lost hands felt for the perceived mistake from the night before. Sadly, the creature still not living rested on the portion just below the belt line. Last night had happened and the plan still must go on. As my second eye opened that's when reality hit that I was no longer a solo show, everyone that I had desired to avoid now gazed upon the situation with a questioning discontent that surfaced in the means of disapproving facial gestures.

Gasping with hands up the town folks would have disapproved of the flowers blooming that day if this moment was detected sooner. I sat a little straighter, focusing intensely on who the leader might be. Nothing the of the encore seemed to give the tribe an appearance of thought. Slowly setting the small remains down on the right with deep breaths pairing with each move I looked around at the audience and out of fear slightly opened a mouth that dropped the small Little Betsy to the ground.

The watching crowd looked ghostly except for a

few, tucking small triangular cigarette packages into deeper pockets. Overall they were shocked in the hands of the perfect. Nothing had happened as such in a thousand years, let alone a human being found alone in the woods with a dead animal. Questions arose but more rampant was the desire for answers. Why, how come, who, what, really and most importantly are we too late?

Stockpiled a rapid confusion gifted the willing a thrill. There was nothing anyone could do but perceive a dead turtle on the lap of an out-of-towner. Death meant pre recollection could thrive as an alternative to fear. After all this was a town of flowers dictated to time while good actions and services were traded in the absence of greed. Loss, especially of a non-human mission was unheard of let alone by the means of a mortal man. The disbelief hung around until bravery found a young enough soul to transmit the question roaming through the green pastures.

"Sir," echoed the young person who originally found me, "How did this turtle die?" Panic roamed and wrapped the sentence in small circles until the need for an answer wielded from a conclusive silence. It was clear that the time to stop beaning and start dancing had arrived. I had been in hard spots before and this was just another tough situation. Standing, I brushed off the falling leaves from well worn outside clothing and spoke.

"Little one, come here closer to me." With the wall of adults they built a fence and it was clear that the explanation would have to be public, except this time material objects were not for sale. Items are not being purchased but actions descended. A one-liner about quality would not be enough to land commission. To tell the truth would most likely end in defeat as well.

Stuck, the moment between scrutiny that assumed and those that could not tell lasted until dry eyes simply stopped blinking. So the moment hung, a heavy weight above a soft moment that had no solid base. What was there to do besides fear the failure of knowing that Little Betsy's would and had killed the planet and your first love was to blame? Back together the two of you sucked while alive and also when you finally made Earth perfect. Unfortunately either could care less with only one knowing the true outcome. Maybe, it would be better to just run from this situation, hide and never look back at the insanity that was then and is now.

In truth, there are no answers for the brave kid. Nothing to be said about why or for what. Earth's Shipping Yard was there in the start and would be there for the majority of the populace still on Earth. The only difference being that they would know why they are there. Why the great voices tells them what to do every day for eternity. Why killing the Earth is bad and leaving what you love is worse.

A small hair scrunchie hits me in a soft butterfly fashion. The original youngster's prize at the question. "At least tell us who you are," pauses then adds, "weirdo." Not only has pollution started but also so has bullying. Out of appearance human conditions have been reborn. Only this time, blame is simple in that there is only one person alive from 2020.

In this moment, silence walked amongst the crowd in the manner of the Grim Reaper or unpleasant rumor. The people had not been fooled in some time but foolishness still lived on the streets as an unspoken shaming strategy. Even with Utopia in place the human mind cannot reduce the amount of judgment it felt to require in a day. This day particularly as one of their animals was obviously slaughtered by a stranger. Maybe the turtle was already in peril and the person under the tree was simply the first to come across the tragedy?

Still staring down the townsfolk there was only one movement that would free me from this particular dilemma. In careful effort as to not disturb the reptiles body any further a great wave of release shot over the heads of the confused. With that little bit of positive power there is enough residue left on the morning dew to make the case of innocent if not savior of the creatures. Knowing very well that the last title might be a little much, there is hope to turn this witch hunt into a successful resurrection of character. A decongestant breath found words traveling over the thick fog in a bit of an easy course.

"Dear people of this great town, do not be worried. Having travelled from a tremendous many of miles there is news from neighboring towns and tribes. First, they extend their condolences for not reaching out about the pandemic sooner.

They had little information themselves and did not want to cause sadness on your day. That said, surrounding colonies are reaching out in an effort to save the cities. There apparently seems to be an underground group of pleasure rebels that seek to bring back the very goods that killed this planet back in the 2020s."

Shock ran viral over the innocent while long-forgotten emotion returned with a slight revenge. Fear, now disguised the dead cold-blooded animal as self-preservation synced in thought that meant hard breathing. "It's okay," I continued, "we can and will stop the spread of this unwelcome newcomer. All we need to know is, who is producing Little Betsy's and why?" Reaching down and picking up the little shelled reptile, I open its mouth and pulled out a numbered portion of the cigarette. Stepping back with guilt the majority of the audience became less forward while the rest looked out of ignorance.

They for the most part have never seen a cigarette, let alone witnessed one arrive out of the mouth of a creature such as this. Questions started to float out of road miles that better describe themselves to the actions of confusion. Split, either side would not raise a hand or question to the image that was now their enemy instead of the traveler.

96

"What is that?" Called the little obvious kid.
"This, little one, not much bigger than a few sticks is a
Little Betsy or better known in some generations as a
cigarette. They used to plague by the billions until one
day they didn't and you wonderful people started
planting wildflowers on your roofs instead," stopping,
realizing the slip I smiled and started again, kneeling
down in front of the little protester, I held out the stogie
level to youthful eye.

"This, is an object parents used to smoke, in Hell
on fire during occasions of stress or leisure. In short ways
this object was a relic of relaxation, other ways this led to
addiction and sickness. In the worst application this small
collection of paper and leaf brought mass pollution."

In a cracked, nervous voice the little being mumbled, "Pollution, are you sure it was the object and not us? I always make sure to put my toys away."

Leaning back on how far the world had come it was prevalent that Utopia would win over this silly invention but by the age of this radical there was time for setbacks, at least for those gathered around. For in my time was a gift already given last year and that gift had an expiration. Smiling while standing there a great movement of prey and predator changed throughout the event. The only whispers to give feedback for the performance said there was only now to act.

"Listen, good recycling folks, this is only the beginning if we do not make it the end. Go forward and find out what you can about these Little Betsy's. Where are they made? Who's making them and most importantly how can we stop cigarettes from killing another turtle. After all, who's to say this kid is not next? All it takes is for one adult to toss their trash or toy in the wrong place for the next generation to find it's harmful truth. Meet here again at the next rising sun with any information you may have. Together this will be brought to a clean conclusion. Where we will also bury this beautiful turtle in memory and symbolism to never have to grieve over a polluted death again."

With that, people of all ages shot into action. No one there wanted blame or relation to what might be just down the road so everyone left in a hurry. Some even ran out of fear of being found out racing without notice to warn Hayden that her production of goods had to be stopped and that they no longer would work for the Little Betsy movement. Regardless as to why the scenery cleared it did and I was left there secretly wanting to smoke the last of the cigarette still stuck between two ready fingers. Just before the ideas on how the symbol of cleansing could be destroyed a tiny voice popped back into the reality of the moment.

"What do you plan on doing with that cigarette Mr.?" Stuck in a tough spot once again by a slight figure I just looked down at the small protester and strained. It was no use as if there was a use to look at the eyes of a begging dog. "This little stick of tobacco, this is going to save the world," continuing, "you see every great purpose needs a symbol to absorb the cause. In this case, stopping Little Betsy's from polluting the world. As long as we have this cigarette we will have everything we need to be successful in the days to come."

Staring at the small pollution in hand, the little creature grew bored and simply replied, "My aunt makes those on 3rd Street with her book club on Thursdays." Shrugging small shoulders naturally the person skipped off to join the others in what felt more like a migration than movement. Left alone with a dead turtle, a piece of future cigarette and the answer to the problem of this impossible journey that had a practical outcome for the first time in this time and the last. Find 3rd Street and this book club and simply bring the town to stop Hayden and her bookworms. A turn there would be easy. Wait for the time here on Earth to expire then be free to rest for eternity. Until then stay low on the details about anything that might give away the truth. Or even give anyone questions about the truth.

Night started to fall when it hit me that I had been standing for hours at this point. Still under the tree with the company of a dead reptile both wondering what had really happened today. On the ground ants began to gather from the corpse of pollution, finding freedom towards a small hole in the ground surrounded by a tiny pyramid of dirt. With respect to the nature of those second creatures, I picked up the innocent life only to lay its body in tall grass around a stone circle and covered it in flowers. A morning for food is never in question but in this particular situation as the planet was in need there might have to be an exception made.

Tomorrow would bring Hayden and all that follows, so not too much time was given in regret as there would be no greater remorse than losing the planet to a trend that involves the reintroduction of war over products. Tired in the warmth that hugged around the giant tree there was not enough power to resist sleep. Unsuccessful, dreams came flowing in just as they have never left. Demanding actions like standing up or sitting down while in complete seclusion. The practice was unfair but a true reminder of why this all needed to happen now and not later. A clear billboard that posed in the center of the road in an effort to provide strict guidelines that Little Betsy's had to be stopped. As a new consciousness rose with the morning start so would this purpose. For tomorrow was the last day on Earth to shut down Earth's Shipping Yard.

"Get up! Our entire town is waiting for you in the city park." I open tired eyes to see the youngster standing by the tip of worn-out shoes, it seems that my clothing and skin is aging faster than all the others. The flesh now was wrinkling to match the multiple holes forming in the surrounding cloth. Time was obviously out for the time traveler. Interesting enough being out of time was a comfortable feeling. Death had already been a reward and being back on Earth was just as busy as ever. A reset had a peaceful conclusion associated with it.

Looking up the boy was still staring down along with the new sun and curious leaves on the tree. All of nature was watching and waiting on me to stand and accomplish saving them from themselves. Once vertical we said goodbye to the tree and look down nervously at the turtle. The small one in silence handed the larger one a silk bag enchanted with rose oil. There is to be a funeral at the park after the town meeting. So that's where all this blends.

Well sir, maybe for the hard shell but it just might be the beginning. Both nodding their heads and turning to the path that leads to city. "What would you like to talk about," said the short stature. "Tell me what life is all about for young people in this moment. What is Utopia in the eyes of an eleven year old?" After pause there was a giggle, "I would not know sir. The shipping yard sent me to deliver you."

Chapter Four. Part II

On the other side of the battle stood Hayden in her kitchen with the majority of the members from her book club. The argument had grown heated about what should happen next with the Little Betsy Empire. The majority thought they should just stop and let this be forgotten until the pursuers went mute. Others wanted to come clean and inform the public that this product is safe and could never be capable of harming a turtle or any wildlife for that matter.

Hayden, on the other hand was not saying a word. Simply watching her friends fight over the future, slipping back into a memory about how all this started. A book, a simple book that would inspire a group of talented people to make one little cigarette. She knew the day they gave this challenge a name that they had gone too far. Now look, friend yelling at friend over a cigarette. This is supposed to be Utopia, we're supposed to be Utopians. The people of planet Earth who finally got it right and are rewarded all the natural pleasures of life. Maybe what the traveler said had some legitimacy to it, that through the production of this rather simple device, violence would find its way back only to breathe fuel into capitalism.

Perplexed, the smashing of a cup full of dandelion wine on the opposing kitchen wall freed Hayden from the solace of her mind. The book club members had now escalated into violence, picking sides of a battle that had not been started. While a ghost in silence she slips from the kitchen to the greenhouse in the backyard where the operation was being produced. Automatically the exact idea of what was going on inside faded. Talking out loud, "How could these plants be so evil in the hands of intelligent people?" Lighting a small flame Hayden lit the frame of the green house on fire.

Walking back to the fight, to friends who were rolling on the ground pulling each other's hair and repeating ancient insults. But in a calm air Hayden spoke, "Listen up everyone," pausing, "I said listen here you charlatans." The room grew calm and everyone including the people on the floor paused in place, walking over to the window and opening it, black smoke filled into the occupied kitchen. There was a rushing to the backyard by the members watching as dark smoke danced with red flames into the sky. One of the book enthusiasts yelled, "Our greenhouse!" Another started to cry. At this point flames had grown to twenty feet high while reaching for other sources of fuel.

The rest of the town, the little one and myself can see the smoke in the distance. In a matter of moments the entire city was heading down 3rd Street in a fury. Before long Hayden's backyard concealed every human from a hundred miles. All just standing there in a circle around the massive fire. The sweet smell of tobacco mixed with fear filled the air. Some started coughing uncontrollably while others ripped off their clothing to make masks. Even with all this chaos no one left. The site tugged at their confused eyes. Destruction of this nature only came from nature and today was a clear spring moment. Gathered, the crowd stayed until only red ash sparked along the ground. A burnt square where the greenhouse was now looks like the outline of a coffin.

Giving enough time for a respectful pause, the little one stepped forward to where everyone could see, "This is where we should bury the turtle." Holding up the velvet bag with both hands in a way that felt more like an offering rather than a funeral. An old man made his way through the crowd with a shovel and started to dig without a word. Others begin to collect flowers while the poet sat and wrote out the eulogy.

With the whole dug the little one went up to Hayden and handed her the bag. Walking over to the hole surrounded by flowers Hayden kneeled with sorrow to place the small creature in its final place of rest. Pushing the dirt back in place with her hands tears fell on top of the freshly scattered soil. Standing, she turned to face the town, "It was," pausing, "it was me who-" Being cut off by The Traveler, "I killed the turtle."

The crowd moved away forming a space around the guilty individual. "Yes, it was my doing that ended that innocent life. I was growing tobacco in the woods. My body was tired so, I rested on the tree for a smoke. Upon Awakening the murder had already gone down. The cigarette must have fallen from my hand and the turtle ate it. Everything that has escaped out of my mouth has been a lie or attempt to protect myself."

In complete confusion the surrounding people just stood there with mouths open. Using this shock I slowly made haste from Hayden's backyard aiming for the country road that leads to the tree. Everyone eventually came to some sense and then began to dissipate into seeing whispers of the last rumor. Before long the grave site was empty besides Hayden and the little one. Both sitting on the step looking at the stone marker by the turtle. Hayden turns her head smiling at the little one. The little one turns to gift the gesture, "We saved him." Nodding Hayden replied, "Yes, we did."

106

Now resting back under the oak tree I began to reflect on this journey to Earth. If not for being an outlaw it might have been nice to spend more time here. Taking a deep breath, a calm came with the idea that Earth would continue to move forward as a Utopia for all. With the closing of heavy eyes, the time traveler went into a peaceful dream.

Art by Theresa Rykaczewski

Other titles by Author
Todd Rykaczewski include:

Word Revolt

The Folklore Behind Shade

Masters of Revels

Joan & The Man

To my wife, parents & friends